Peppa Pig™

Pedro's Pirate Treasure

Peppa and her friends have
dressed up as pirates.
Danny Dog is on board his pirate ship.
"Are you ready to play?" he asks.

"Yes, we arrrrrgh!" everyone cheers
in their best pirate voices.
Pedro Pony guards the pirate ship,
while Danny, Peppa, Suzy Sheep and
Freddy Fox search for treasure.

First, Danny finds a pine cone.
"Treasure! Woof!" he barks.
Then Peppa finds a shell, Suzy finds
some rope, and Freddy finds a pebble.
Everyone loves playing pirates and
searching for treasure!

Woof!

Meanwhile, back at the pirate ship, Pedro starts to feel sleepy. He takes off his glasses and falls asleep against a tree trunk . . .

Zzzzzz!

"BOO!" cry the pirates, creeping up
on Pedro and waking him up.
"Oh!" gasps Pedro, surprised. "Sorry, I fell asleep!"

"We've got treasure to put in the treasure chest,"
says Peppa, showing Pedro.
Everyone puts their treasure on the ground.

Pedro guards the ship again, while the rest of the pirates head off to find a place to bury the treasure.

Over a hill and round a little bush they go . . .

Hoooraaaaaaahh!

"Let's bury it here!" cheers Danny.
Freddy digs a hole. Danny puts the treasure
chest inside and covers it with soil.

Peppa draws a treasure map. "Over the hill, round the little bush and 'X' marks the spot!" Danny draws an 'X' on the ground to mark where the treasure is buried, and the pirates head back to their ship.

When they get back, Mummy Pony
arrives to collect Pedro.
"Stop!" shouts Pedro, guarding
the ship. "Who goes there?"
"I'm your mummy," says Mummy Pony.
"Where are your glasses, Pedro?"
"Oh no!" says Pedro. "I think I put them
in the buried treasure chest."

"We can find them with our
treasure map!" cheers Peppa.
Mummy Pony uses Peppa's map
to find the buried treasure.
"Over the hill, round the little bush . . .
and 'X' marks the spot," says Peppa.

Peppa's map leads them straight to the treasure. After Freddy digs it up, Pedro looks at it very closely . . . "My glasses!" he cries. "Hurraaaaaahhh!" everyone cheers.

"Treasure maps are very useful," says Peppa.
"Especially for finding glasses if you
accidentally bury them!" adds Pedro.
"Ha, ha, ha!" everyone laughs.

Hurraaaaaahhh!